MOONLIT MIRAGE

A COOK ISLANDS ROMANCE

AMY MCKINLEY

ARROWSCOPE PRESS, LLC

Moonlit Mirage (A Cook Islands Romance)

(*p*) **ISBN-13**: 978-1-7339425-7-7

(*e*) **ISBN-13**: 978-1-7339425-6-0

Publisher: Arrowscope Press, LLC; www.arrowscopepress.com

Editing—Taylor Anhalt, Editor, Kate B., Line Editor, Taylor A., Proofreader, Red Adept Editing

Cover Design—T.E. Black Designs; www.teblackdesigns.com

Interior Formatting & Design— Arrowscope Press, LLC; www.arrowscopepress.com

1

CADE

A loud crack sent a shot of adrenaline through me as a vehicle swerved into my lane. My hands tightened into a death grip on the steering wheel. There was no movement to my car, no change in how it drove. It must have been a rock from the other car's tire. Rather than risk an accident, I eased off the accelerator while crossing the bridge. The surge of energy slowly dissipated, and I again fought to stay alert.

"Rise Against" by Savior blared from my speakers, and I tapped my finger against the steering wheel to the beat. With a slow blink, I took my gaze from the road for a split second and lowered the windows to let in more of the cool August air, which I hoped would help me remain awake. It had been hot as hell during the day, but by nearly midnight, the temperature had dropped to a chilly sixty degrees. I was glad for it.

Despite my intentions to leave at a reasonable hour, I'd stayed at my dad's company to finish some extra work for my grad-school internship, which meant I'd fulfilled my requirement. It was a relief, but all I wanted was to fall into bed and sleep for hours.

After the bridge—and I was almost at the end—I wouldn't have much farther to drive to get home.

Light glared in my rearview mirror from an oncoming car. Averting my eyes, I concentrated on the road, staying in my lane. They were coming fast. The bridge had two lanes bound to Long Island, and I was going slowly enough that they could go around me.

Chills swept down my spine and along my arms, awakening a sixth sense of some sort, and I glanced again in my rearview mirror. *Shit.* The car was flying, barreling down on me. I punched the accelerator. It didn't look like they were going to change lanes. Sweat broke out on my forehead as they rode my bumper. My grip tightened on the wheel. *Come on, pass me.* I was going seventy miles per hour. *If they hit me...*

Their turning signal went on, and I almost sagged in relief. They were going around. *Goddamn.* That scared the hell out of me. I was suddenly wide awake.

I maintained my speed. I heard the roar of their engine as they punched the accelerator. *Whoever that is must be drunk.* My gaze switched from my mirror to the road in front of me.

The car shifted to the left, leaving my lane. My grip on the wheel didn't ease. There was nowhere else to go, and it was too late for me to switch lanes with them straddling both. The guardrail was on my right. *Come on.* With excruciating slowness, they inched partially into the next lane, far too close. I pushed the accelerator down, giving them more room to get over.

The blinding light in my mirror eased, and a minuscule amount of tension left me. I could see them inching to my left from my side mirror. I kept up my speed, so close to the bridge's exit. Once the other car moved over, I would ease off the pedal, but not yet.

Metal crunched in a cringe-worthy explosion. The world spun as the wheel jerked in my hands. Pain lanced across my chest as the seat belt bit into me and locked tightly. Tires squealed. My head crashed into something. I fought for control. The car spun anyway. My vision tunneled at what was ahead. There was nothing I could do. The car slammed into the guardrail, and the airbag deployed only to deflate with a hiss. *Shit, the rails*—they couldn't withstand the impact of a car going this fast. *Please hold.*

It didn't.

I was trapped, held in place by the seat belt, staring out the side window. Then the car tipped. My stomach dropped with the car as it fell. I could only watch in horror as the car rushed toward the East River.

The impact of hitting the water was like a second car accident. It sounded almost like an explosion as the car collided with the river. Water instantly poured through the tops of the windows as darkness smothered my vision. I felt warm liquid trickle over my eye as the car slowly sunk. My heart was beating a million times faster than it should have been. With my right hand, I struggled with the seat belt. *Do not panic.*

It was stuck.

Water flooded into the car from the partially lowered windows. I was screwed. I didn't think the car that hit me had stopped. No one was coming. So late at night, the traffic wasn't heavy. I clicked on the overhead lights as a biting cold lapped at my knees.

Someone will stop. I had to believe it. The car kept sinking, and I struggled. With more room, I pushed at the seatbelt button then yanked on the strap as hard as I could. *Who made these things?* It didn't budge. I fought with it while gasping for breath. The water was at my chin and climbing. I took a deep breath then ducked underneath the surface, searching for anything to cut the belt away.

I wouldn't last much longer once the car was fully submerged. I tipped my head back, elongating my spine. My lips cleared the waterline but barely. I took in as much air as I could. My lungs burned as I yanked hard on the belt, but nothing happened.

Movement on my side of the car spiked a thread of hope, and I turned my head in that direction. The light from one of my headlights illuminated someone swimming toward me. I squinted through the inky darkness. It was a woman—no, a girl, maybe. She was small. As she neared, her dark hair billowed around her heart-shaped face. Her forehead creased, and I tugged at the belt so she would understand that I was stuck. My lungs burned. A small burst of air bubbled from my lips. *Am I hallucinating?*

This is it. I couldn't hold my breath much longer.

She positioned herself with her hands on the door handle and one foot on the side. Then she kicked the half window of glass. Her heel made contact with a clink of something metal, and glass shattered and floated around us. Not wasting a second, she reached inside and manually slid the lock to open. My mind was chaos. More air slipped past my lips. She gave a hard tug, but the door stayed shut. I tried too. Nothing happened.

She left my sight. I strained to see where she went. *Please don't leave!* But I didn't want her to die down there too. The car stopped sinking when the front end hit the river's murky bottom.

When she reappeared, the last of the air I'd been able to hold escaped. Half her body fit through the open window. I went to gasp, but she grabbed the back of my neck and then fit her lips over mine, like a seal. I fought to stay calm. She shoved her tongue in my mouth, and tiny zaps of electricity exploded through my body at her touch. There were worse ways to die. I went with it.

My eyelids drifted shut, and I let myself feel her softness. My fingers ached to be buried in her hair, but I didn't want to scare her or for her to think I'd hold her down there as she ran out of air too.

I parted my lips at her insistence, intent on taking over the kiss when she pushed the air from her lungs into mine. With a tap against my chin, my slow brain processed what she was doing. I couldn't waste the gift she'd given. My eyes opened, and I closed my mouth, holding in the precious oxygen. She pushed away from the open doorway.

She'd bought me time by sharing her air until help arrived. I could only assume she'd left to get someone. I looked up but didn't see her ascending to the surface. *Where the hell had she gone?* My mind had latched onto her rather than my predicament. She looked younger than me. *Had to be seventeen? Hopefully eighteen? God, I hope she made it out.*

When she reappeared, my brows furrowed. I waved my hand to the surface. She shook her head. Once more, she grabbed the back of my neck and fitted her lips over mine. I didn't waste time with confusion. She fed me oxygen. It tasted flat, stale, but my straining lungs greedily accepted it.

I leaned as far as I could and glimpsed her feet by the front tire. *That's where she was getting the air? Smart.*

As I waited for her to return, my mind spun. *Is she the one who'd hit my car? Had to be. Why else is she here, helping me so soon after I'd gone over the bridge?*

When she returned, I looked her over. There wasn't a scratch on her. She was beautiful, ethereal. I committed everything I could to memory in the dim glow of my interior lights.

A faint sound echoed through the water. Her hands gripped the side of my face, and she forced more air into my mouth, more than last time. Unable to stop myself, I lifted my hands and cupped her face. Her touch left me. There was a tug on the strap holding me in place. The belt gave away, then she broke the seal she had over my lips. She glanced up, and her delicate features hardened. Twisting, she pushed off the side of the door and swam away in the direction from which she'd come.

Light shone in a beam through the water as I worked free of the severed belt. *Why had she fled?* I glanced up. Red and blue lights danced over the water in addition to the flood-lights in each of the two rescuers' grips. I shoved away from the car and swam upward.

One thing I knew was that the girl had gone, and there had to be a reason for it. The only thing that mattered was that she'd saved me. I owed her my life.

Nadia

MY HEAD BROKE the water's surface as I stepped onto the rocky bank. Flashing lights drew anyone within range to the side of the bridge where Cade's car had busted through and then fallen into the water.

Beneath the water, noise had been muted. Out of the river, sound returned. It was New York, after all, the city that never slept.

He'd been my mark, one I'd let myself get involved with—even if from afar—outside the mission. My fingers pressed against my swollen lips and considered the reaction I'd had to touching him under the water. It'd been to keep him alive, nothing more. But it was so much more, and I was shocked.

He wasn't for me, if anyone was. I had a job to do, and there was no time for foolish thoughts.

Relief coursed through me in a steady stream, mixed with anxiety over the next part of my mission. Darting my gaze around, I emerged from the river once I caught sight of the icy blonde, Hannah. She was a defector-flipped-sleeper-agent who scared me to death but had also offered salvation. With her help, I had a chance to escape.

I slogged through rock and mud until I stood before the small grouping of trees where she waited. Just out of view, I joined her within the cover. My teeth chattered, and she handed me a blanket. After I wrapped it around myself, I willed the physical discomfort away. Her icy gaze narrowed. I knew what she was thinking. I was better than that—I shouldn't let the temperature get to me. I had been trained by Russian operatives, and I could withstand much more than a short duration in chilly water.

Squaring my shoulders, I met her gaze with determination. I let her see the steel inside of me. I could do it. No emotion flashed across her face, and I schooled mine to match.

"Did you get them?" she asked.

At her clipped, no-nonsense question, I notched my chin. "Did you stop them?"

If I hadn't been staring so hard, I would have missed the minuscule tilt of her lips. I'd amused her. That was better than anger. She awarded me with a brisk nod. All the fight left me. The two people I'd lived with for the past twelve years were no longer my problem.

"And the girl?" I asked.

"She's safe."

I dug in my pocket and tugged the keys loose that I'd swiped from Cade's car. I dangled them between us. Her fingers closed around them before she dropped them into the purse at her side. "Let's go."

A burst of hope shot through me. *This is it.* For my assistance, she would take me away from there. I couldn't help myself—I took one last glance toward the bridge. Then I turned, shedding the life I'd had and the obsession I'd developed for the person I was supposed to kill.

2

CADE

Five Years Later

I took another sip of Irish whiskey, savoring the smooth, sweet taste while sitting outdoors in the cool tropical night. Bongos pounded out a beat while the islanders performed a traditional dance. Grabbing dinner and catching the show hadn't been planned, but I was glad I'd come. It was a nice change from working in my room or relaxing on the beach. I'd been island hopping during a much-needed diversion from life in New York. Once on Rarotonga, one of the Cook Islands, I'd decided to book an extended stay.

October in the South Pacific was a far cry from home. The steady rain had ended before my plane touched down, and since I'd arrived, there'd been nothing but sunny days. Relaxing there had been great, but I was tired of my own company. My sister wasn't due to visit for a week or so.

Stars decorated the sky that evening, and I'd been alternating from picking out constellations to watching the dancers in grass skirts on the stage. Flames from the Tiki torches beat back the inky darkness, their light surrounding the large crowd, who'd come to experience a night filled with island tradition. The buffet had held my focus a while before, thankfully. Drinking whiskey on an empty stomach wasn't the smartest thing, and I'd welcomed the Uma food, prepared in earthen ovens the resort used to cook several native dishes.

A dancer wielded a twirling flame, capturing the guests' attention along with mine, until the soft glow highlighted a woman standing near the stage. I leaned back in my chair and openly stared. There was something familiar about her profile, but I couldn't place her. For the next few minutes, I alternated from the show to her, until I couldn't look away any longer. Long dark hair tumbled down her back in loose waves. When she turned, I could see the outline of her heart-shaped face and plump lips. Time fell away, and I drudged forth the memory of the woman I longed to see again, super-imposed over her profile. My heart kicked into overdrive. *Is it her?*

I'd sworn I wouldn't think of her anymore, the girl who had saved me the night of my accident five years earlier. After looking for her in every female face who had even the slightest similarity, I'd forced myself to let go of the obses-sion. I wasn't going to find her again. Nor would I experi-ence the same spark for another that her touch elicited—I'd tried.

I couldn't squelch my need to know if it was her. That woman looked exactly like a slightly older version of my underwater angel. Before I knew it, I was out of my seat and crossing to where she stood near the stage.

The same questions from that night whirled around in my mind. *Who was she? Why had she left?* I had to know.

Then there was the kiss. Of sorts. I was calling it a kiss. My gaze never left her as I weaved through the audience and the filled tables. Like me, she wore a long-sleeved T-shirt and shorts.

"Excuse me." I kept my voice low so as not to cause a disturbance to the show. She turned her head, and it was as if time stopped. *Holy hell, it's her.* Five years before, in the faint glow of my sinking car's interior dome light, I could only tell her hair was dark. It had grown. Beachy midnight curls fell almost to her waist. I wanted to reach out and touch her creamy sun-kissed skin, experience those soft-as-sin lips against mine again. Her eyes were a brilliant blue, framed in thick lashes. She was stunning, even more so than the girl who'd haunted my dreams. I cleared my throat as she appeared to wait for me to say something.

"Do you remember me? The night of the accident?" I couldn't help it. I had to know.

Her pupils flared. Otherwise, she gave no indication that she did. With a shake of her head, she said, "No. I'm sorry, I don't believe we've ever met before."

"My apologies." My heart plummeted. Inching my foot to the right, I almost turned away, but those alluring blue eyes kept me there. I would try another way. The flame twirler's show ended, and someone stepped onstage to announce the conclusion of the evening's entertainment but added that the night was still young and the buffet and drinks would be open for another hour or so. When conversation rose around us, I leaned closer. "Can I get you a drink?"

"Sure." Her lips curved into a small smile. "I'd like that."

With my hand on her lower back, I guided her to my table and ordered her a vodka tonic. I glanced over at her. She appeared to be at ease, but some sixth sense told me she was on edge. I'd guessed she was hiding from the police when she didn't stay after the rescuers dove in—maybe she'd been afraid I would turn her in. There was no way I would have done that.

The busy waitress placed her drink at the table. After she'd taken a sip, I eased into a conversation with her. "I'm Cade."

A slight nod, then, "Nadia." She had an American accent, another clue to her origin.

"Do you live here on the island, or are you visiting?" I asked.

"Who wouldn't want to live here?"

Her smile momentarily stunned me, and I raked my hands through my hair.

"What about you? Vacationing with family?"

She hadn't answered my question. It was her. I was sure of it. "Just me. I've been island hopping for the past few months and decided to remain on Rarotonga a while longer. Nothing about this place gets old."

"So true." She swept her hand in the direction of the resort. "Is this where you're staying?"

I nodded. She wasn't wearing a ring, and there wasn't a tan line or indent. "It is."

"They offer a lot of amenities. It's one of the best places to stay here."

"I agree. I've done everything the resort offers in terms of water sports and hanging on the beach. This week, I want to explore more of the island."

"I'd recommend it. There's something magical about this place."

There was—it was where I'd found her again. "Are you staying here as well?"

"No." One of the dancers waved to Nadia, and she returned the gesture.

"Are you here with one of the performers?

"I came to watch some friends, but I should be going. I have an early meeting in the morning."

"Of course. But if you don't mind, do you have any recommendations for what I should do tomorrow?"

"Oh." She took a sip of her drink. "Depends. If you want an adrenaline rush, I'd recommend cliff diving or zip-lining. Maybe a tour or hike to see the waterfalls?"

"That last one sounds perfect, but only if you go with me after your meeting. Or are you here with someone?" Silence stretched between us, and I swear her eyes hardened. *What is she thinking?*

She stood, pausing by the side of our table. "I can take you."

My gut eased with the confirmation that she wouldn't slip through my grasp again. "Then it's a date."

3

—————

NADIA

He doesn't know. I adjusted the straps on my compact, waterproof backpack, took a deep breath, and went over to the area by the resort's pool where we were to meet. I was early. And nervous—something I didn't experience often.

I'd checked with a friend who was a maid there. After I'd described Cade and given her his last name, Malone, she'd confirmed he was a guest. What I couldn't understand was how he'd found me—if he was, in fact, looking. I frowned as I searched the guests for anyone who didn't appear to belong. There were two ways I could go about things: I could confront him or trust in fate for once.

This could be my chance. I dropped into one of the recliners and made myself comfortable for the fifteen-minute wait. Again, my gaze skimmed over the sparse number of guests swimming or settling onto pool chairs, always searching.

No one raised an alarm. Meeting someone I'd just met wasn't usual for me there—the place was my oasis. It offered the anonymity I'd craved when I'd first arrived. If I reconnected with Cade, everything I'd worked for could implode.

No matter how much my common sense screamed to run, I couldn't. Not from him.

As much as I could, I had steered away from the more touristy places, except for yesterday. I shouldn't have given into my friends' insistence to watch them perform. The one time I hadn't kept them at arm's length, and they'd pounced. I shouldn't have been involved with anyone or gone to the show, but I was glad I had.

From the moment I'd first seen Cade five years before, he'd invaded my thoughts. I'd left that life behind, for the most part—my subconscious hadn't gotten the message. More often than not, he was in my dreams, and the memories of the touch of his lips and his hands as they'd cupped my face were still strong. *Had he felt the same thing?*

Probably not.

A rebellious part of me, the one that by some miracle survived all those years, yearned for a shot with Cade. I asked myself what the harm would be. I knew the risks. Even so, I was a fool for the guy.

With the area cataloged, I slipped my backpack off and rested my head on the seat. Staring a hole into the resort's door, I drummed my fingers on the mesh chair before crossing them over my tense stomach. A warm breeze swept through, carrying the scent of tiare maori, the island's flower.

I'd worn a pair of jean shorts and a sports bikini top. My thick hair was secured in a messy bun, and sharp, metal hairpins added decoration. The day promised to climb into the upper eighties, and we would be hiking for a while to reach the waterfall.

The door opened, five minutes earlier than he'd said we should meet. Everything in me stilled as he zeroed in on me. Awareness of his intense gaze skittered across my skin, and I was glad I'd worn sunglasses, as I'm sure my eyes would've betrayed how he affected me. Plus, it gave me a moment to appreciate his appearance, as every female in the near vicinity was doing.

I rolled to my feet, grabbed my pack, and secured it over my shoulders. I had everything I'd need in there, and the hairpins, in case things went south. I hoped they wouldn't.

Cade was the one who'd gotten away by my design, which meant I couldn't have a future with him no matter how much I wished things were different. I was so thankful he'd been the turning point and that I could help him, which also changed everything for me.

"Good morning." His deep voice reverberated along my nerve endings, and I fought a full-body shiver.

"Morning." Technically it was, but at eleven, I'd been up for hours. It felt more like early afternoon. "Ready to go?" I took in his board shorts and a gray T-shirt that molded to broad shoulders and a tapered waist. Either my memory wasn't doing him justice, or he'd filled out, gained muscle. He'd only been twenty-two all those years ago, so I wasn't sure if I didn't remember correctly.

He stopped in front of me, and I lifted my chin to meet his gaze. At five foot five inches, I wasn't short, but he had to be six-two and towered over me. I'd taken down larger men, so I wasn't worried in case I'd misjudged his intentions. Plus, I had everything I would need in my bag if our meeting was somehow predetermined.

When he reached for me, I tensed. The slide of his fingers at my shoulder, slipping under the strap of the backpack sent a rush of heat through me.

"You're prepared." His green eyes sparkled. "I can carry this."

"No thanks. It's light." I didn't trust him yet, so that would be a hard pass. With a step back, I put some space between us and plastered a smile on my face. "Ready to go?"

His brows furrowed, but he nodded. "Lead the way."

We exited the resort he was staying at on the southern portion of the island and stepped onto a trail that would take us to the falls.

"I'm surprised you haven't been yet," I said.

"I finished a project for work yesterday, so I have time to do more now." His long legs matched pace with my shorter ones.

"What do you do?"

"Mostly coding." He held aside some dwarf-palm fronds that had invaded the path for me.

"Are you self-employed?" I found myself holding my breath, waiting for his answer.

"I am. I code and do consulting work on a contractual basis for larger companies. It gives me the freedom to travel if I want to. What about you?"

I shrugged, not wanting to lie. "You mentioned you've been traveling for a few months." The sound of the falls grew louder with each step. "Do you have somewhere to go back to?"

"Not anymore. I had an apartment in New York, but I wanted a change."

He didn't say why or who he could have left behind, and I dropped it. "We're here." I pointed, hoping he would drop the topic, as I didn't want to share anything about my past. We stepped onto a rock overhang with a fantastic view of the cascading water. Several minutes passed in silence as we took in the sight before us. It was one of my favorite places on the island. "Want to swim?"

"You mean jump from here?" A grin flashed across his face.

A twig broke behind us, and I whirled around, scanning our surroundings. Leaves rustled near the base of a tree, and I relaxed when the small animal scurried farther into the underbrush.

Cade's arm brushed mine when I turned back, and I shifted away. He noticed.

"Nadia, is everything okay?" Concern swam in his eyes, and he reached out, his fingers lightly touching the side of my hand.

I didn't pull away but let the sparks that seemed to ignite from a mere touch have free reign. When I met his gaze, I recognized the look. I wanted to tell him that his concern wasn't from what he thought, but I couldn't share that with him. Not everything. "I'm fine." I offered a small smile. "We don't know each other."

Several seconds passed as he looked at me. I felt as if he could see into my soul, and I shivered despite the oppressive humidity.

"We may not have learned each other's names before last night, but I know you, Nadia."

"How can you? We met last night for the first time. You see the outside package." My heart kicked up in gear at how true those last few words were. "Let's jump." I moved away from him and shimmied out of my shorts. After unlacing and kicking off my shoes and socks, I took a chance and dropped my pack to the side. I had the hair ornament should I need it. When I looked back at him, I almost stumbled back. He'd removed his shirt. *Yeah, he gained muscle.*

We jumped at the same time, our arms spread like wings. Warm water welcomed us, and soon, we kicked toward the surface. When we came up for air, he grabbed my waist and pulled me close. Laughing, I held onto his shoulders, feeling no threat in his touch. For once, I wanted to let myself go and be normal, if there even was such a thing.

He'd moved us near the far bank to a spot where he must have been able to stand. The water would be over my head, so I let him hold me up. But it was his crystal-clear green eyes and the depth of emotion swimming in them that held my focus.

"What you said on the overhang, it's not true. We may not have known each other all those years ago except for one impactful night. Every time I close my eyes, I meet you again in my dreams. I see *you*, Nadia. There must be a reason our paths have crossed again. And this time, I'm not letting you get away. We're not in New York, and I don't care who you were running from."

I melted at his words, and when he pulled me even closer, my legs automatically went around his waist. "Why do you assume I was trying to get away from someone?" There was no point in pretending we hadn't met. I wanted him. For once, I wanted someone for me.

"Ah, you admit we know each other." His voice deepened. "And I think that because you didn't stick around when the rescuers dived in with flashlights. I assumed you were avoiding the cops, or that you were the one that crashed into my car." His thumb traced the small indentation near my hairline and frowned. "And this? Did you get this scar that night?"

I brushed his hand away from the crescent mark. "Nope. It's just an old scar. And I didn't hit you that night." That much I could share. "I wasn't running from the police, either. I knew you'd be okay when they dove in and didn't want the hassle of being questioned."

He nodded. "None of that would have mattered anyway. I want to get to know you, Nadia."

Slowly, he closed the distance between us while the roar from the falls filled the air, matching the frenzied beat of my heart. My fingers slid from his shoulders to the back of his neck. With the first brush of his lips, my stomach clenched. He teased me with the gentle back and forth caress until his hand cupped the back of my head, tilting it to the side, where he could gain better access. The touch of his tongue urged me to open for him. I sighed into the kiss, all awareness of where we were fading.

He controlled the kiss, molding me against him. For once, I let go, giving control to another. I was helpless in his hands, dizzy from the desire he'd coaxed to a raging fire inside me.

To an emotionally deprived woman, it was everything.

I PACED along the length of the pool outside of my small villa, wondering what I had been thinking. For the hundredth time, my fingers brushed across my swollen lips. Hannah had been the one to bring me to paradise. I didn't want to jeopardize what she'd done for me, and reconnecting with my last mark in New York could very well do that.

I flopped into one of the chairs by the small waterfall that fed into the pool then sucked it up and tapped Hannah's name on my cell to call her. I had to come clean, especially with all she'd done for me. She picked up immediately, and my stomach tightened even more. "Hannah, it's me, Nadia."

"Is everything all right?" Even from Maine—I was assuming that's where she was—I snapped to attention at her icy, commanding tone.

"Yes. At least I think so." Deep breath. "Cade Malone is here... and he remembers me."

"Do you need an extraction?"

"No. I'm okay." My fingers drummed on the chair. I was going for it. "He thinks I helped because I was the one who hit him or witnessed the accident and couldn't risk getting involved with the police. That's all he's said, and I believe him. I-I want to stay here."

Silence stretched on the line between us, and I waited for her to say something—anything. I should have told her he was interested in me, but I wasn't ready. I would take it one step at a time. Because if she said I had to leave, I didn't have a choice but to listen to her. I owed her more than I could ever repay.

"I want to know what he's up to, Nadia. If he had any involvement with his father or his father's associates, then you're in danger."

"He was questioned. I thought he was cleared." I bit my bottom lip to stop from saying more.

"You and I both know how to pass interrogations, lie-detector tests. It would be foolish of us not to be sure, and I don't want to risk your life. There are other places you could go if your location proves to be compromised."

Don't get attached. It was a cardinal rule, one I'd broken twice. Cade—he too was in my dreams each night, no matter how much I tried to forget him. And the island had become home to me, and even though I could do it, I didn't want to leave. I'd grown a lot there, freed from the chains that bound me to my birthplace. That meant something.

"What do I need to do to be sure?" I'd spent hours investigating him the night before, and nothing I'd found raised an alarm. From what I could tell, he was clean. But Hannah would want more, and she would be right—she usually was.

"Gain access to his personal computer. From what I've learned, he keeps one that he does not connect to the internet. It's secure, locked down tight. I want to know what's on there. Download everything."

"I can do that." A shiver coursed down my back. I could break into his room while he was at the beach or pool. That was the smartest course of action.

"Check back with me within the next twenty-four hours, or I'm coming there."

I relaxed against the chair, relishing her concern, which meant the world to me. "I'll be fine."

She sighed, and I could imagine her rolling her eyes or shaking her head. "I know you can take care of yourself, Nadia. You aren't alone anymore, and I'll be on the jet if anything is wrong. You like him. I can hear that in your voice, but I want you to be safe. I'm doing what I can here to triple check everything we've got or can find on Cade—I need to be sure too."

"Thanks, Hannah. I'll check in soon." After I disconnected the call, I dropped everything onto the chair and dove into the pool. My arms cut through the water, and I focused on increasing my speed after each open turn. No matter how much the island felt like paradise, I could never let my training suffer. Thirty laps later, I sank to the bottom, watching the minutes tick by on my waterproof watch. At twenty minutes, my lungs were screaming. After another sixty seconds, and I was kicking to the surface, gasping for breath as soon as my head cleared the water.

I knew I could do better. Others could. German free diver Tom Sietas held his breath for twenty-two minutes. I vowed that I would beat that someday.

Memories battered against my mind as I eased to the edge of the pool. I crossed my arms on the deck and rested my cheek on them, allowing those twenty-five minutes underwater with Cade from years ago to come forward.

In leggings and a tight shirt, I'd kicked off my shoes at the edge of the tree line before stepping into the chilly East River near the end of the bridge. I could see Cade's headlights approaching. My source had said he was a few minutes away, but I knew the car trailing him wouldn't pick up speed yet. It would soon, though, and I needed to be in position. I maneuvered along the bridge, swimming until I was close to where it would happen. Those few minutes could have meant everything to him.

Beneath the bridge, I treaded water and waited. The

sound of cars crashing exploded into the night. Tires screeched, then the metal-on-metal shriek as his car slammed into the guardrail, busting through. Headlights careened through the night until one sped away and the other arced toward the water as his car fell from the bridge.

That was my cue. I took a deep breath and dived under. It would have been a piece of cake if he wasn't injured, but as ordered, I'd rigged his seat belt and knew he would be trapped.

The car sank fast. Following the headlights as it hit the bottom of the river, I closed the distance. Cade had the windows halfway down, and water filled the interior. I could see him struggling, attempting to get free of the tight seat belt. He couldn't. There was no give from the harness.

The overhead light was on as Cade jerked on the belt. His eyes went wide as he caught sight of me. Some of the precious air burst from his lips. I had to hurry—I didn't want him to swallow water. I got the door open, glanced at his belt again, then dived to the tire. Unscrewing the cap, I rigged the pin so air would escape. I took lungfuls and turned back to Cade, grasping the back of his neck and pulling his mouth to mine. With one touch, I was reeling. I'd wanted to do that from the moment I'd set eyes on him during surveillance. But he wasn't mine.

My mouth had sealed over his, and I had to focus on the steps so as not to lose myself in the feel of his lips. I hadn't been panicked, but he was—at least at first. My tongue had traced along the seam of his lips, and he opened. Taking advantage, I fed every ounce of air I could hold into his mouth. When I'd given all I had, I urged him to close his lips tightly again. I pushed away before his hands could move and swam to get more oxygen.

Back at the open car door, I grasped onto his shirt. His panicked features had calmed somewhat at my touch. He'd thought I'd left him—I could see it when I returned. That wasn't the plan, or at least not my goal. Several times, I repeated the process of giving him oxygen. Near the end, he'd reached up to cup my face. I forced myself to stay present. Focused on our connection, he wasn't watching where my hands were. Grasping the keys from the ignition, I twisted them until they released. I secured them in the waistband of my pants then pulled the knife free from beneath my shirt.

Lights were flashing above, and I'd registered the rescuers diving in, the yellowed beams bobbing in the murky water. With a hard slice to the belt, I severed it. Once he'd closed his mouth, sealing the air in, I pushed away and disappeared. I couldn't stay.

No matter how much I'd wished it, I wasn't a normal girl.

4

———

NADIA

The shrill beep of my alarm jolted me from sleep. My hand slapped down to shut it off as I blinked into the inky early morning hours. It was two in the morning, and I had things to do. After dressing in black, I padded across the wood floor in bare feet to my gym shoes. The whirl of the fan above my bed was the only other movement in my small villa. With the silvery light from the moon, I didn't have to turn on the lights. Everything I needed was within reach.

My gun was secure at my back, and the small pack with tools for the lock and the flash drive were in my pocket, along with the electronic device to break his password and gain access to the computer. Hannah's friend Chris had made sure I had any tool he thought I might need when I'd settled there.

It didn't take long to arrive at the resort where Cade was staying. It was one of the best on the island, and even at two in the morning, I knew I risked being seen by staff. That didn't matter—I would make it work. That time of night offered the chance of running into fewer people than during the day. I kept my head down and moved quickly through the lobby, into the elevator, then once on his floor, to his door.

The hallway was empty and silent. Withdrawing the electronic keycard that Chris had assured me would grant me access to any hotel or resort rooms, I held it up to the electronic pad. With the click of the lock and its green light, I eased the door open. No lights were on, and I slipped inside, shutting the door with care. He had a large suite and thankfully wasn't in the main part but in a room off to the side. It was time to find his computer.

Penlight in hand, I searched the room. The granite counters in the small kitchen were clean and empty. The coffee and end tables didn't yield any results, either. *Shoot.* I would have to go into his bedroom. He probably kept the computers close by.

The door was a few inches open, and I clicked off the light before approaching. Standing at the cracked doorway, I waited, listening. The sound of Cade's slow, even breathing mingled with the whirl of a fan.

Inside his room, I crept to the edge of his bed. Weak light spilled across his bed from a gap in the curtains, catching his angular jaw. Asleep, his features looked softer, peaceful. A single sheet covered him to mid-chest, and I wanted to slip under the covers and curl against him.

I shoved those thoughts aside. After a quick sweep of the room, I found two computers on the dresser beneath a widescreen TV. With no idea which one was his personal computer, I disconnected both without making a sound and crept into the main room. I powered them up at the same time, hitting the volume buttons to silence them before any noise could wake Cade.

It didn't take long to determine which laptop wasn't connected to the internet. With Chris's device, I was able to get past Cade's passwords. I plugged the flash drive into the USB slot, and I got to work copying the contents to peruse at home. I shut down the other computer and took it back into Cade's room, reconnecting it precisely as it had been.

I had several minutes to wait for the content to download. Unable to resist, I went through the room, looking for anything personal. It wasn't until I neared his bed once more that I saw the pictures. I focused on one of his mom and sister. I'd seen them before. That was all there was—nothing with his dad or a significant other. Taking care not to make a sound, I riffled through the drawers in case there was anything else that would incriminate him, such as a gun or a passport under another name. I ran my fingers along the doorways and checked the floor, under the bed, or anywhere there could be a hidden compartment. I took longer than I needed for the information to download. I had to be thorough—I had to be sure he wasn't a part of that other world.

When I was out of places to search, I disconnected the flash drive and shut the computer down. When it was back in its place, I found myself at the edge of his room, hesitating. There was another place to look, but I didn't dare. Behind the dome lights was a great place to hide something, but that was for another night. My instincts said he was clean, and I wanted to believe them more than anything. If he was involved in the world I'd escaped, I would likely find something on his personal computer.

In the same manner I'd entered his room, I left. It would be a long few hours until we'd agreed to meet again in the daylight. If he was clean, I vowed to go to him as a regular woman who didn't have a closetful of dangerous baggage.

THE SUN WOULD BE up soon. With a final sip of water, I

jumped off my deck and jogged down the dark path I knew by heart. Five steps in, I increased my pace to an all-out sprint, pushing myself as if my life depended on it.

That was key.

I stayed focused on my breathing, footfalls, where to go, but a tiny portion of my mind drifted in the pre-dawn air. Soon, the island's natural humidity would blanket the land like a hug from an old friend. The part of my mind that I allowed free reign wandered, despite my focus on reaching the water in less time than it had taken the day before.

From every possible angle, I ran through scenarios as to why Cade was there. After stealing the contents of his hard drive and vigorously going through them, I wanted to believe his appearance on the island was fate and nothing more. After turning over the data to Hannah, I let it all go, including the suspicion, the urge to flee, and even holding myself back from the what-ifs between us.

I was going for it.

It was my one chance at creating memories with the only boy who'd broken through my shields. I wanted it, and I was going to let it happen as if there weren't secrets between us— dark ones that could ruin everything.

Kicking my shoes off, I sprinted into the water until it was deep enough that I could dive in and swim farther out. When I reached the point I wanted, I inflated my lungs with as much oxygen as I could then swam to the bottom. The large stone was in the same place as it was every morning. Sitting cross-legged on the seafloor, I tugged the heavy weight in my lap and counted the minutes as they ticked by on my watch.

Putting my former life behind me was one thing, but forgetting the training was suicidal, no matter how much I liked to pretend it wasn't.

Being underwater gave everything a dreamlike quality,

and I let the peacefulness of it seep into my chaotic thoughts. If I could, I would have stayed longer. As it was, my lungs burned from those few seconds, which I counted on my watch's backlit digital counter: twenty-two minutes. The rock tumbled onto the ocean bed in a cloud of disturbed sand as I pushed toward the surface. After a few powerful strokes, I burst free of the water, sucking air. Once my heart settled, I kicked off to the shoreline.

It didn't take long to grab my shoes then walk the rest of the way back to my villa. I had plenty of time to eat breakfast, shower, and take a short nap before I was to meet up with Cade.

When the shrill sound of the alarm went off, I got up, feeling refreshed. Dressed in a white bikini, I tied a sheer wrap around my hips. My backpack was already packed, a different one that time—it was smaller and waterproof, and I'd loaded it with drinks, sandwiches, sunscreen, and out of habit, a few hidden weapons. My hair was again twisted on top of my head in a messy bun with a Celtic cross copper hair fork secured in it. Slipping flip-flops onto my feet, I slung the pack over my shoulder and headed out to meet up with Cade.

Along the walk, I had time to think about what I'd been doing after breaking into his room. He had programs he'd coded on his personal computer, and they appeared that he was developing them to sell them, rather than trying to get a business contract. At least that was the impression I'd gotten. I'd gone over the coding, the notes, the plans for the projects, and his expectations. To me, it seemed legit and that he was doing things the way he was to safeguard against theft from a hacker. It was smart.

I'd done what Hannah had requested and sent her everything. Chris would comb through all the data and give us the final summary. For the time being, I was moving forward as if Cade was clean. Besides, he was only visiting, and I could see no reason why I shouldn't enjoy the time I had with him until he left. Nothing would come from it but satisfying the obsession I'd developed when I was seventeen.

I couldn't have him then. But I had my chance, and I was taking it.

On the beach, I looked out to the small coral inlets. There were four of them. Our plan was to hang on the beach, explore, and maybe check out the small island that was accessible by walking, maybe doing some minor swimming during low tide. That's what he'd seemed most interested in when I'd suggested it at the end of our time together the day before. I paused to look across the water, waiting on the beach in front of his resort. He would join me soon.

"Hey." Cade spoke from behind me.

He was outside sooner than I'd thought. Chills danced along my skin, and I shivered from the effect his deep voice had on me. He laughed, running his hands up and down my arms as I turned to face him.

"How can you be cold? It's almost ninety."

"I'm not," I admitted, but I didn't step away from his touch. "You startled me."

"Are you okay?" He frowned, and I rolled my eyes.

"Didn't sleep great. It's nothing. I promise." There was no doubt in my mind he'd seen the dark circles under my eyes that I hadn't bothered to fix with makeup. I didn't see the point. We would get wet, and he would see them anyway.

His gaze wandered, even as he spoke. "I hate even to suggest this because you look amazing in this bikini and I like spending time with you, but do you need to grab some sleep?"

"No, I'm good." I shoved him and started to walk to the shoreline. He looked unsure, so I threaded my fingers through his and gave him a carefree grin. Tension eased from his features, and he returned my smile, tightening his grip on my hand.

"Do you want to try for the small island across the lagoon over there?" I pointed to the one I was thinking about. It wasn't far and would give us time to get to know each other.

"Yes, I wanted to explore that, but it didn't hold the same appeal, doing it by myself. It's beautiful here."

The sun climbed the sky, warming everything in its path. The tropical air was hot and humid but comfortable. I'd lived on Rarotonga for five years, grateful every day that I did. With Cade, I saw the island through fresh eyes: the beauty, freedom, and absolute paradise at our feet.

Colorful fish darted away as we waded into the lagoon. The farther in we went, the higher the water climbed. It was high tide, not low, and we would have to swim soon. We pointed out interesting fish to each other as we walked. The water level was up to my waist. I would need to swim. "Ready?" I asked. "It's not too far, but I forgot to ask if you're a strong swimmer or not."

"I can manage." He glanced at my backpack. "Won't that get wet?"

"Well, yeah." I rolled my eyes, enjoying that I could joke with him. Everything wasn't serious for a change. It was refreshing. "The outside."

"Smartass." He hooked a finger under the strap at my shoulder. "I can carry it."

"I do this all the time. I'm used to it. Besides, what's in the pack is essential. I'm not sure I trust you with it."

A speculative gleam flashed in his eyes. "Essential, huh? I should probably get a look inside before we go any farther," he teased.

"Too bad you won't." My response was light and flippant but also based in truth. I wouldn't let him riffle through the stuff I brought.

He reached for the bag again, and I laughed, hopping away. "If you want to know what I have in here, you'll have to catch me." I dove under and pushed off the sandy floor, and the water dragged against the pack. When I surfaced, he was hot on my heels, his arms extending too close to my kicking feet. A thrill rushed through me from his chase. With practiced ease, I increased my strokes. Halfway to the uninhabited island, I chanced a look. He wasn't too far behind, but I couldn't help but tease him. Treading water, I yelled, "Sure you got this?"

He slowed at my shout then stopped and treaded water when we were beside one another. Light danced in his green eyes. "I thought I was in shape until this."

"Well, I am a lot younger than you. I can see how your old age is the problem."

He cupped his hands and shot a spray of water at me.

Laughing, I swam a little farther away. "What are you, like thirty?"

"Close. Twenty-eight, but something tells me you already know that."

I wasn't biting. "How could I? We just met and haven't had the age discussion." Before he could respond, I dove under and kicked away. I would rather have had that talk on the shore. After a few strokes, I checked back to ensure he was following. He was.

The sandbar stretched several feet from the small island, even during high tide. Not in a rush, I touched down, my feet digging into the sandy floor, and I waited for Cade to catch up. He'd proved to be a strong swimmer, and I wasn't worried about him. It had been a good distance for someone who didn't spend hours in the water regularly.

A foot away, he found his feet and trudged closer, sucking in air. I grinned. He reached me, and I patted his flexing abs

—something I'd wanted to do before we'd got in the water, and asked, "Doing okay?"

"Such a brat. But I should expect that. You're what, nineteen?"

"That would make you a cradle robber, wouldn't it?" We made our way to the white-sand beach.

He groaned. "That would ensure I was only your friend."

"Can't have that." I was bold but going for it. "I'm twenty-two."

"That's better, I guess." An uncomfortable look crossed his face. "Still makes me feel like you're a kid."

That, I'd never been. "Please. You're six years older than me."

Dropping my pack onto the sand, I unzipped it and pulled a thin, dry blanket out. He helped me spread it, and we both fell to our knees while I tugged the bag closer. "Sandwich?"

"You weren't kidding about needing this. Thanks." He took the proffered food from my hand.

I set two water bottles between us, and we let the silence settle as we replenished the calories we'd burned with lunch. He finished eating before me and seemed lost in thought. I waited for it—he had questions. They would come soon.

"That would have made you seventeen when you'd saved me that night."

There was no use denying it, and he didn't know everything. "Yes."

"Why didn't you stay? I wouldn't have pressed charges if you were the one who ran me off the bridge."

"You were right." I offered him a sad smile. "There was something I was running from. I couldn't risk talking to the police, even though I wasn't the one who caused the accident." He opened his mouth, and I placed my hand on his leg.

"It was another lifetime, one I've left behind. Let it go, please?"

A few seconds passed before he nodded. "I understand about starting over."

"Ah, you're running from something too?"

A sand crab scurried away, and he followed its sideways path. "Memories mainly. The last few months have been freeing."

"While you island hopped?" Part of me wondered if he was looking for me. I vowed not to ask.

"Yes." He met my gaze with eyes shrouded in pain. "The accident. That was the start of a much bigger nightmare for my family. As much as we could, we've moved on. There isn't anything holding me in New York any longer."

"No job?"

"I don't need to visit clients, so I can work anywhere I want."

"I do the same. Gotta say, I love it." I wouldn't press him for details I wouldn't have shared if asked. I stretched back on the blanket, content. The sun warmed my skin and evaporated any lingering drops of water. The moment he lay down beside me, a thousand butterflies set flight in my stomach.

"It had its advantages. I've been looking for a new place to settle, to call home. Rarotonga is a strong contender."

I turned my head and squinted at him.

Propped on his elbow, he studied me. "It's where you are."

"You don't know me." My heart kicked up a notch, thudding against my rib cage.

"I'm trying to."

He hooked my backpack with his index finger and set it on my other side then closed the distance between us. When he lowered his head and his lips brushed mine, I let go of our surroundings, of who I had been, of who I was, of who we could be—I wanted to live in the moment. Sparks flew between us as he parted my lips and swept his tongue inside my mouth. His chest rumbled with a growl as he settled fully on me, and I welcomed his weight. My arms looped around his neck, and I toyed with the hair at his nape. Heat built between us, and I wondered how far we would take it. When he broke from my mouth and trailed kisses along my jaw and down my neck to pause, breathing deeply, my eyelids fluttered open, and I cradled his head. He paused, sucking in air as we both struggled to regain control.

"I don't want to go too fast." His rough voice rumbled from his chest. "You're driving me crazy, but I want to get to know you."

When he tilted his head up to meet my gaze with desire-filled eyes, I cupped his cheek, my heart swelling. "I'd like that too." I gave in to the dream of what could be.

5

CADE

After tossing the wrapper from a sandwich I'd grabbed from the restaurant downstairs, I finished the last few lines of coding. That was that for the day. I had to get out of those rooms. The resort was amazing, but I was tired of living out of hotels.

Four days before, Nadia and I had spent the day together exploring the uninhabited island across from one of the lagoons—and each other. Getting to know her solidified what my subconscious had tried to tell me all those times I'd dreamed of her… She was the one for me. How I'd known back then was a mystery. There had been a physical connection from the first touch, but there was so much more.

She'd taken a few days off from her work, as had I. We went kayaking and wind sailing and zip-lining before that. I liked spending time with her. We had a lot in common physically, but that wasn't all. I was comfortable around her and felt as though I could reveal my darkest secrets and she would accept me regardless. I wanted to, but I also would rather have left the demons where they were, in my past.

But I had a surprise to share with her. After a quick pass

around the room to make sure I hadn't forgotten anything, I shut my laptop down, grabbed my wallet and phone, then headed to the door. My cell rang as I stepped over the threshold and into the hallway.

"Anna," I said, recognizing my sister's new number right away. "Anything wrong?"

"No. Not at all. I'm ready to get out of here and have fun at the beach. I was calling to make sure you were still expecting me."

I shook my head. "Ah, I invited you here." The doors opened. I got off the elevator and headed in the direction where I was meeting the realtor.

Anna laughed. "Right. Okay, I'll see you in a couple of days. I can't wait."

"Me too. It's been a long time since we've hung out."

We said our goodbyes, and I made a mental note to call Mom the next day. Maybe they would both come out for Christmas.

I only had to walk a short distance. Pocketing my phone, I waved to the realtor, who stood on the empty expanse of land. We were on the southern side of the island, where it was quieter—not as close to the airport, but the island wasn't huge, so it would be fine.

Fifteen minutes later, the realtor left with electronic signatures, and I waited for Nadia to meet me there. For the first time in five years, I felt everything inside me settle. All the confusion and anger melted after setting foot there, and especially after finding her again. If it wasn't fate, I didn't know what was.

"Hey." Nadia's hand landed on my arm as she appeared beside me.

"Hey, yourself." I bent down and pressed a kiss to her lips. "I didn't even hear you get here." She moved so silently that it was eerie sometimes.

"So…" She glanced around.

"Right." My nerves sprang to life, despite my prior conviction that it was the right thing to do. "What do you think of this spot?" It was up on a slight elevation, with palm and a few other fruit-bearing trees spread across the plot of land. The view was incredible. A short walk without any other obstructions, and we would be on the white-sand beach.

She bounced her gaze from one area to the next then turned back to me with furrowed eyebrows. "It's beautiful, but I don't understand what you're asking."

"I bought it."

Her big blue eyes flared, which wasn't the reaction I'd been hoping for.

"It'll take about six months to build, at least."

A smile curved her plump lips, and the tension between my shoulders eased as she seemed to snap out of her shock.

"It's a perfect spot. Congratulations."

I accepted her hug but pulled back so I could read her expressions, at least the ones she showed. She was surprisingly adept at hiding how she felt unless we were having fun. Everything else, though, was harder to determine. "Quite a twist of fate."

Turning, she made her way down the path to the beach. "What is?"

I followed, wanting to push her a little to gauge her reaction to my plans to stay. "We've found each other after all this time." It felt like it meant something, and I wanted her to admit it too. "The one place I've visited over the past few months of travel finally seemed like home, enough that I wanted to settle here."

"It is paradise," she said.

She toed the water, and I moved next to her. Our fingers entwined. Despite how much I liked to spend time with her, there was much I didn't know. "I haven't even been to your home. I bought the land because I want to be here, but is it upsetting you?"

"You surprised me is all. I was convinced we had a short time together. This is good news, Cade."

"Is that why you've kept me at arm's length with where you live? And your past?" She had been less guarded over the last few days than she'd been when we'd first met, and it gave me hope.

She shifted so that we faced one another. "No. I did it so that I wouldn't get too attached." A small smile curved her lips. "But it's too late for that. Come on. I'll show you where I live."

It was a start. More tension slipped away. I wanted whatever it was that grew between the two of us. We were on foot, but the island was small, only about thirty-two kilometers. It would have taken us a mere forty-five minutes to drive the entire circumference by car.

Hand in hand, we walked along the beach, and when the reefs made it necessary, we moved to paths nearby. "How far is your home from here?"

"I'm on the north side. It's not too much longer."

"Do you like it there?" We didn't live as close together as I would have liked, but maybe in time, she would move in with me.

"Yes. Your spot is better, but I've been happy."

With a tug of her hand, I followed her up a path from the beach. Thick foliage banked either side of the trail. The trees shielded us from the sun until we came upon a small villa. She lifted a panel near the door and entered a code then pressed her thumb against a fingerprint-recognition pad. A bolt slid back, and she turned the handle then pushed the door open with a silly grin. "It's high tech."

That alone appealed to me, and I made a mental note to do something similar with mine.

"One of the things I do for work is design security. It's not needed here on the island, as there is little to no crime, but I'm a bit of a geek that way. Plus, I don't need to carry around a key."

It made sense, and I was happy she'd shared something personal with me. I wouldn't have guessed that she was a computer geek too.

Once inside, I looked around at the open-floor plan. The ceiling was high with wood planks, beams, and a large fan that circled in a lazy whirl over the living room and kitchen, adding a sense of charm. The furniture was sparse but inviting. I followed across the dark hardwood, past the high-end kitchen, and stopped in my tracks at the rear of the house.

"Wow." A wall of glass separated the inside from the pool out back.

She laughed, clearly pleased. "You're staying at the most expensive resort on the island, and this gets that kind of reaction?"

With a shove, she opened the wall of sliders so the house merged into the backyard. The pool was long with a water-fall flowing over a rock grouping at one corner. Two lounge chairs cozied up to the water but remained under the house's overhang. All along the back was the thick surround of the jungle. It was picturesque and beautiful, and I wanted to hang out there every night with her. "The resort is great, but this is private. You can't beat that."

"Want something to drink?" She went back inside to the kitchen.

"Yeah, thanks." I dropped to one of the chairs then noticed the rolled-up mosquito netting that surrounded the short overhang. The place was perfect, and I couldn't help but upgrade the ideas for my own spot to include a pool and lounge area similar to hers.

I took the coconut water she handed me and tilted it back for a sip as she sat nearby. "How long have you been here?" I asked.

"A few years."

I lifted her legs from her chair, as it was so close to mine, and draped them over me, wanting the connection of skin on skin. She was evasive, which made me want to work harder to get her to trust me. "So not long after we met for the first time?"

She winked but didn't answer. I was taking that as a yes.

"Do you have a roommate, or is this place yours?"

"I own it. I bought it before realizing I might want to be closer to the southern end of the island." She shrugged. "It's home now, and I love it."

"I can see why." My thumb traced lazy circles over her thigh. "How many bedrooms?"

"One. I didn't want a big place. Still don't. This is the right size for me."

"So you work out of your bedroom?" I couldn't imagine having an office in the room I slept in. I knew she worked from home but not what she did or for what type of clients. Either way, it seemed she was able to work remotely, as did I.

"Rarely. I have a laptop, like I assume you do, so I work wherever I want. Usually, it's out here." She pulled her legs back to her chair and bent her knees. My hand followed, resting on her outer thigh. With her chin settled on her knees, she nibbled on her lip for a few seconds. "Did you buy that land because of me?"

"For the most part, yes."

"We haven't known each other that long, Cade. I'd hate for you to invest so much money then find out that whatever this is between us is short term."

Most girls I knew would've jumped at the possibility of a long-term relationship, especially if they had an idea of how much I was worth, but she was cautious and didn't know about the money. I didn't flaunt it, except for the places I booked to stay in when I traveled. I had to be honest for her about my feelings because I doubted she would first. "I'll admit I want to explore what's between us. You've got to agree it means something that we found each other after all this time."

A midnight curl fell forward, and she tucked it behind her ear. "I think there's a reason too. Maybe it means we have a second chance, one without the ties from our past."

Her leg was taut with tension beneath the touch of my hand. It was clearly important to her to maintain old secrets, and it wasn't too bad a deal for me. Eventually, I would tell her about my family, but maybe not so soon into our relationship. For a chance with her, what she asked was a no-brainer. "Yes. No ties from the past."

Hours later, after we'd eaten dinner on the resort's outdoor patio, complete with twinkling lights beneath the darkening sky, we strolled along the shoreline. Hand in hand, we stopped to admire the moon's silvery path, which seemed to beckon to us across the ocean's surface. I didn't want this night to end.

* * *

Nadia

"How do you do it?" We swayed from side to side on the beach, the faint strains of the band carrying to our secluded area. His breath feathered across the top of my head as I rested my cheek to his chest, secure in his arms.

"Do what?"

"Make everything so easy. If I hadn't witnessed that car accident, I never would have thought anything bad ever happened to you." There were very few shadows in his eyes, but a part of him had to have that died that night.

He slipped his fingers into my hair, cradling my head against him. "The crash was so many years ago. I survived, thanks to you. As for things seeming easy, I'm not sure what you're referring to."

"Moving here. Building." *What does that mean for us?*

He stopped walking and tilted my head back, so our gazes met. "It wouldn't matter where I was, now that I'm with you. Ever since that night"—he shrugged—"we connected without words. I can't explain it, but I never forgot you. I dreamed of you. Now that I've found you, I won't pass up the chance to build a life together."

His lips brushed across mine, and I relaxed against him. Warmth spread through every part of me he touched, and I lost myself in his hands even as my one fear battered against the edges of my mind. *Will he still want me when he knows that what we had was built on a lie?*

6

NADIA

I laid the blanket over the sand where it kissed the edge of the tree line on Cade's new property. We'd agreed to meet there for lunch, and it was his turn to bring the food. The day was gorgeous, and I settled on the ground and lay back with my head resting on my crossed arms. A yawn stretched my mouth wide, and I flexed my toes before getting comfortable again. I was early, and after a long night of researching Cade yet again, I was sure of the decision I'd made to let the past lie where it was. That would make a fresh start, one I wasn't going to pass up.

The cadence of the waves breaking along the shore made me drowsy and relaxed. On the island, I'd found peace, at least enough to let my guard down somewhat. As the minutes ticked by, the familiar language of the ocean lulled me to sleep.

My body reacted the instant I felt a touch to my arm. Fight mode surged through my veins as I latched onto the hand at my forearm, twisted, and launched on top of the potential threat, my other hand around his throat. Air sawed in and out of my mouth as my vision cleared from a red haze of danger to one of horror.

Cade was sprawled out beneath me while I straddled him, one hand pinning his to the ground, the other tight around his throat. *Shit.* I lifted my hands as if his skin was on fire. "I'm sorry." I rolled to my feet and backed away a few steps.

"What the hell was that, Nadia? You wake ready to fight?" He sat up and rubbed his neck before he looped his arms around his bent knees, making no move to approach.

"I'm not used to anyone waking me. Not for years. It's an instinctual reaction, and I can't tell you how sorry I am." Heat flooded my cheeks.

Seconds ticked by as he seemed to absorb my explanation. "Are you okay?"

"Just embarrassed. Did I hurt you?" I dropped back to the blanket and reached for him but second-guessed the gesture, and my hand hung in the distance between us.

"I feel as if there's something more." He raked his hands through his hair then grabbed my hovering one. "I get that you want to keep the past where it belongs and not bring up whatever it is you ran from. I'm fine with that."

The pause after what he'd said let me know he meant "for now." *Can I live with that? I want to.*

"We're getting to know each other and looking forward, but I have to know if someone hurt you and that's why you reacted as you did, if you're hiding and worried that very person will find you."

"No." *Not in the way you're thinking. Or even who.* "My fight-or-flight reactions are a bit extreme. I should never have taken that self-defense class." I rolled my eyes and laughed in an attempt to lighten what I'd done. He'd clearly assumed that I'd run from the cops, and that was the reason for my behavior, and that had grown into worry that someone had physically hurt me. I relaxed my shoulders as I watched the tension ease from him at my explanation.

"I won't keep asking because I get it. We're starting fresh, but you can talk to me." His voice was husky and melted my heart even more.

"I hear you." I squeezed his hand. "Thanks."

With a smile, he reached over to the bag he must have set down before touching me, as it was intact. "I cheated and ordered food from the resort."

"That works." I took the utensils and container with ika mata, raw fish mixed with chopped vegetables and coconut milk. My gaze skimmed over the land and toyed with what his new home could look like. "What are you thinking about for your house?"

"I want to take advantage of the view."

"So a wall of windows? What about a lanai?"

"Yes, that's a must." He took another bite and chewed. "I like the setup you have in back too. I'm playing around with designs of what I want before I meet with the architect next week."

We ate as we talked. Anything I didn't finish, Cade did, until there was nothing left but the containers.

"Well, you've got the ocean anytime you want. Are you sure you want the maintenance of a pool?" I liked having both but had no idea what his vision was.

"I like the ambiance. For indoors, I want three bedrooms and an open floor plan to take advantage of the view."

"Makes sense." We packed away our food containers, and I took a risk. "If things don't work out for us, will you regret having a house here?" I planned to talk to Hannah later. I wanted to tell him everything.

"Are you doubting this?" He gestured between us, and I shook my head. "I won't have any regrets, Nadia."

I hoped he would think that after I told him why we met underwater all those years before.

"I WANT TO TELL HIM." I paced back and forth in my living room, my stomach a bundle of nerves. "There wasn't anything on his hard drive."

"No. It was clean." Hannah paused. "But it's not safe. I understand why you want to tell him, Nadia. I do. You shared your feelings with me when we had our little chat. But emotions aside, if he knows, then you're at risk."

The chat she mentioned had actually been an intense interrogation. I'd spent days at her mercy—her condition to ensure I wasn't hiding something and wouldn't turn on her or those she cared about if she helped me to defect and begin a new life. I'd shared everything I'd felt about Cade, including that I was attracted to him and that I wanted something for myself for once in my life, and that was him. If anyone knew my motivations, what I felt, it was Hannah.

I spun on the ball of my foot and pushed off into the opposite direction. There wasn't enough space in here. My body vibrated with the need to run or swim laps. "I get what you're saying, I do—"

"What if he told someone connected to his father? You and I are aware of the risks. Is telling him worth the danger of being found?"

"At this point, yes." I stopped at the glass sliders and gazed out the back, over the pool and the chairs where Cade and I were not long ago. "I want to have a real relationship with him, and what chance would I have with everything based on a lie? *You* have that. Jack knows everything."

"He didn't. Not at first. When we were dating, he had no idea who I was. The circumstances here are different from how Jack found out. How do you think Cade will react if he learns you weren't there to save him that night? Or that you knew who ran him off the road and why?"

With a shove, I opened the sliders and sat on one of the outdoor chairs, staring off into space. "What can I do?" The thing was, Hannah wasn't giving me the okay to tell him, and I worked for her. The specifics of my past and future were woven together with hers.

"You can have a relationship with him based on who you are today, not who you used to be. I won't deny you that. The details of your past, even the ones that converged with his, need to remain there."

"And if something slips?"

"You're better than that."

I was. Our training hadn't been that different. "I hear you." Nothing could change.

"Nadia, enjoy what you have with him. That's real, isn't it?"

It was so very real.

7

NADIA

I smoothed my hand down the front of the sundress I wore to meet Cade's sister. She would be there for a few days only, but he wanted to take me to lunch with them. Over the past several weeks, we'd only gotten closer. The framing of his house was underway, and he'd consulted with me on everything. He wanted me to move in with him, but I kept wondering if it was too soon.

My fingers drummed against the side of my leg. I knew I could rent out my house. If things went well after meeting his sister, then I would do it.

A knock sounded at the door. I grabbed a small purse and headed out. "Hey."

"Hey yourself." Cade grinned back then leaned in for a kiss. "You look gorgeous."

"Thanks." For a change from a bathing suit or shorts, I wore a sundress that ended at mid-thigh. I shut the door behind us and laced my fingers with his. "Where's your sister?"

"She's meeting us at the restaurant."

We meandered down the path and headed toward his

resort. I had been so nervous about coming face-to-face with his sister that I had straightened my hair and left it down. It fell in a long curtain around my shoulders and back. "What's your sister like? Older, younger?"

"Anna is two years younger than me. We look a lot alike, but that's where the similarities end."

"Really? She's not athletic or a geek?"

He chuckled. "I want to be offended, but since you're one too—"

"So true." I nodded, completely serious. He and I had a lot more in common than he thought. "What about the rest of your family? Will they be visiting soon, or when the house is done?"

"I'm hoping my mom will come for Christmas with Anna, but she's in a new relationship, so I'm not sure."

"Oh, your parents are divorced?"

"Uh, yeah."

"Will your dad visit separately?" I had to ask. That's all I needed to know, for the time being.

"No. What about you? Does your family come for the holidays?"

"I don't have anyone. It's just me, so no."

He looked surprised, so I squeezed his hand to let him know I was okay with that. And I was, more than he knew.

"Well, you'll like Anna. She won't do a lot of the activities we like, but she'll hang on the beach and shop."

"I'm sure I'll love her." It was her reaction I worried about.

We rounded the side of the resort and entered near the back. The restaurant overlooked the ocean. With a hand resting on my lower back, Cade led me to the indoor one, not the more casual one with tables situated under umbrellas, which was fine but fancier than I expected. Maybe that was how Anna liked things.

After weaving through a few tables, we stopped at one

with a classy looking woman whose chestnut hair was cut in an angled bob to frame her pretty face. It was a becoming look and accentuated her eyes, which I already knew would be the same shade as Cade's.

"Nadia, this is my sister, Anna."

Cade made the introductions, and his sister tipped her head back to greet us both. For a split second, her features froze. *No. Not now.* I plastered a wide smile on my face and extended my hand to her. "It's so nice to meet you. Cade has had nothing but wonderful things to say about you."

That distracted her enough so that she glanced away from me to her brother. "Hm, I'm sure."

"Come on, Anna. What could I possibly have said that wasn't flattering?"

She giggled and leaned back in her seat. "Fine. You're off the hook. I already ordered an appetizer." Her slender hand rose in the air, and she signaled for the waiter.

After we placed drink orders, she turned her focus back to me. "So, Nadia, how did you and my brother meet?"

"Here on the island." I spoke before Cade could. "I'd promised friends I'd watch their performance, and it happened to be one where Cade was in the audience. He introduced himself then, and we've been hanging out since."

Anna nodded, a half-smile on her face. "Are you vacationing too?"

"No, I live on the island." I maintained a calm, pleasant expression, and she seemed to relax.

"That brings me to another thing I wanted to tell you, Anna," Cade interjected. "I'm building a home here. I'm not going back to New York."

"Well, I can't say I blame you." Her shoulders slumped. "Moving away from there was the best thing I ever did."

"Where do you live?" I asked her. "Someplace warmer than New York?"

She smiled. "Can you tell from my tan? I went to graduate school in Georgia and never went back."

The waiter deposited our drinks and appetizer. Anna fidgeted with her glass, turning it with her fingers. "I don't think I've met anyone Cade has dated since high school."

"Where are you going with this?" Cade scowled at his sister.

I laughed, enjoying the awkward moment between them. "This sounds interesting. What kind of girls did he date?" Elbow on the table, I rested my chin on my hand and grinned at his sister, hoping to start a little banter between them.

With an eye roll at her brother, who tried to redirect the conversation, she laughingly said, "Cheerleaders. He was on the football team, and they were all over him. Oh, I'm sorry." She frowned. "Were you a cheerleader? I wasn't thinking."

"Ha! No, I was one of those nerdy girls who nobody saw. Completely invisible." I scrunched up my nose and mimicked her eye roll. "I'm not offended, I promise. Tell me, what did they look like? Did he have a type? Blondes?" I wiggled my eyebrows at Cade.

"Now that I think about it, no. But he wasn't a typical jock, either. He was a huge nerd, too, although you'd never really know it because everyone focused on his athleticism. I was a lot like you in high school. Invisible."

"We'll always have that." I winked at her. "Look at us now. We're not doing too bad."

"True." She paused in the nervous twisting of her cocktail glass. "You look so familiar, Nadia."

Shit. I shook my head. "I'm sure it's my hair. With how dark it is, I look like a native." There was no point in saying I was born here—I knew she could hear it in my voice, and I hadn't adapted an accent when Cade and I had reconnected, so…

"I don't think that's it."

"They should have another island night tonight. Do you want to do that, Anna?" Cade asked.

The breeze blew several strands of hair into my face, and I pushed it back. Anna jerked, spilling her glass. I froze, my hand holding back my hair. Horror washed over her features.

Her gaze locked onto my exposed hairline, and that's when I knew that she'd recognized my scar. Somehow, she must have seen it before.

Cade hadn't noticed yet. He grabbed a few napkins and was sopping up the amber liquid that spread over the table, threatening to drip into his lap. "Ah, Anna. A little help?" An ice cube rolled off and landed on her. She never moved.

Tears streamed down her face, and her entire body trembled. My hand fell, giving in to the wind and hopefully obscuring whatever it was she recognized.

"It's you." Her voice, a thready cry, caused Cade's attention to jolt to her.

"What are you talking about?" he snapped, and I broke my stare with her for a split second.

Anna stood with her finger extended, pointing at me. Her features twisted in anguish, and hysteria was obviously close. "You—"

"Stop." Although quiet, my voice cracked like a whip, and she responded. Her mouth slammed shut while her body shook like a leaf. "No talking."

A whimper escaped, and her eyes widened impossibly at the slip.

"What the fuck, Nadia?" Cade snapped at me, clearly horrified at his sister's distress.

"Take her to your room." I wanted to reach out to him with a need born of its own, but there would be no way he would accept my touch, not anymore and probably not ever.

I stood and took a step backward. The words I had to say

to him tore from my straining throat, leaving a bloody trail as they hit the air. "Goodbye, Cade."

Anna collapsed into Cade's arms in a mess of silent sobs.

I turned and left, unwilling to see the hatred that would fill Cade's eyes when he realized why his sister feared me.

It was over.

8

CADE

What the hell is going on? I'd managed to get my hysterical sister back to my room but hadn't been able to make her talk for over an hour. Once she'd calmed down, she gripped the glass of amber whiskey like a lifeline. An occasional shudder wracked her thin frame, and I adjusted the room's temperature again.

Unlike Anna, my anger heated my body, even more so after I left a furious, half-yelling message on Nadia's voicemail that said she'd better not go anywhere. I said I would be by her place that night or the next morning to hear what the hell she had to say and that she'd damned well better be there. The fact that she hadn't answered sent a confusing mix of frustration and worry through me. Because for as much as I wanted to, I couldn't turn off my feelings where she was concerned.

I tossed my phone onto the dresser in my room and went to check on Anna, who was in the same place I'd left her in, on the couch in the suite's main room. The low hum of the air conditioner mixed with Anna's sniffles. I'd drawn the blinds, and the soft glow of a table lamp was at her elbow, the only additional light in the room.

The last thing I wanted was another breakdown like the one Anna had just had, but I needed answers. Part of me that didn't want to admit that Nadia had anything to do with my sister's past rose up and shook the walls of my mind. *Please, don't let it have been her.*

"Anna, I need you to tell me what that was about. How do you know Nadia?" I kept my voice calm and low.

She sucked in a few stuttered breaths, her knees drawn tightly to her chest. With a blanket wrapped around her shoulders, she looked frail as she huddled in the corner of the couch. "She looked different."

"Nadia?" I leaned forward, my forearms braced on my thighs as I waited for her to tell me more.

"Back then, she had tight blonde curls that barely brushed the tops of her shoulders." Anna took a shaky sip of whiskey. "I never saw her eyes. She wore big sunglasses all the time, and they swallowed most of her face."

"Why do you think this person was Nadia? And what about her caused that reaction?"

"It was the scar," Anna whispered. "I noticed it once then when her hair had this small part in the curls. I could see the crescent-shaped divot. It was the size of a fingernail. Nadia has the same scar in the same shape near her hairline."

I rubbed my palms over my face and pushed back in my chair. I couldn't say my sister wasn't right, as I had met Nadia around that time too. Nadia and I had a lot to talk about. I knew it would be an endless night. "I think you need to tell me everything, Anna. It's been a long time, and I need to hear the details again."

She downed the rest of her drink, and I took it from her hands. With a nod, she then rested her head against the back of the couch. "Nadia was the one who took me that night from campus. It was late, and I was leaving the library. Even now, I couldn't tell you how she got me. One minute, I was walking, and in the next, I had a bag over my head and was blacking out."

"Chloroform?"

"I'm not sure. It happened so fast." With a tug on the blanket, she drew it tighter around her. "When I came to, I was in a room with a bed only. There were no windows. Two doors. Both were locked." Her traumatized gaze met mine. "Trust me. I tried them even with my hands tied. There was a cloth keeping me from making too much noise."

"I remember you telling us and the police that you were there for three days." We hadn't known she was missing until we'd gotten the call that she was at the hospital. She had been away at college, and it wasn't unusual to go a week or two without us contacting one another.

"Dad knew." A spark of life reentered her dull eyes.

I was furious too. That, we shared.

"Nadia came in several times a day to make sure I had food and water. If I had to use the bathroom, she'd take me. I never saw the other two people who were there."

"Then how did you know there were two? Could Nadia have worked alone? Or were there more people?"

"I heard them, Cade. Nadia's voice and two others. They spoke in another language. One I couldn't place. I wasn't even able to tell the police any of the words. It was faint when they spoke or even yelled. The walls were thick."

"Nadia took you because of our father? Blackmail, right?"

She shrugged. "I don't know. She was… not horrible, I guess. I was so scared, and she made it worse on the last day I was there. It was late, sometime after dinner. She'd rushed me into another room. I didn't see anyone because the blindfold covered my eyes again. It wasn't far, where she took me, but God, I was so scared. She shoved me into a closet, and I had to huddle in a small space while she stacked boxes in front of me. It was what she said that made me stay quiet. She told me that if I made any noise at all, even if people were calling for me, I would be killed. She said she was trying to help, but if I wanted to make it out of there alive, I had to do what she said."

"She saved you? But she was the one to take you in the first place." I struggled to wrap my mind around what the hell Nadia had done. Not only that, but she'd found me that night too. I remember because my mom had told me about my sister after the accident. It'd been a nightmare of a day for her. First finding out about what had happened to her daughter and me, and finally, my dad.

"When she stuffed me into that closet, she whispered that they were going to kill me either that night or in the morning. Either way, I had to be quiet so they didn't find me. Then she put an empty box over me and another on top. I didn't make a sound—just lay there for hours, terrified. Then they came, the CIA or FBI or something. They knew where to look, Cade."

For the first time since she started talking, she lifted her head, and another thread of life seemed to infuse back into her—and into me.

Nadia

I COULDN'T STOP the tears, which ran in rivers down my face as I sipped vodka, neat. I should have run the moment he'd spotted me that night on the island, but instead, I was putting not only myself in danger, but Hannah, Jack, and their team, too, or so I thought. I was so confused by my feelings.

A shiver raised the hairs on my arm, despite the warmth of the room. I could fall back on my training, which would get me through the situation. But I didn't want to.

For the twelfth time, I looked over at my silent phone on the table next to me. I'd retreated to the deck, needing any ounce of tranquility that could be found there. Cade's voicemail played on repeat in my mind. Not an ounce of the man I'd gotten to know was reflected in how he'd spoken in that recording—fury bled from his voice. I couldn't blame him. I'd taken his sister, his family. When I put myself in his shoes and thought of him harming Hannah, as she was the closest person I'd ever had to a sister, I saw red too.

Sucking in a much needed breath of courage, I picked up my cell and pressed the button to connect me to Hannah, the woman who'd given me a new lease on life, and who could also order me to leave at a moment's notice, never to see Cade again. If I were to leave, there would be no way for him to find me.

She picked up after half a ring. "What happened?"

Her no-nonsense voice caused me to straighten up and emulate her. I needed to strip my emotions and relay the facts and only the facts.

"Cade knows who I am, mostly. His sister, Anna Malone, is on the island and recognized me from the small scar by my hairline."

"Have the authorities been notified?"

"I don't think so. Cade left me a message that we would talk tomorrow morning. He said possibly tonight, but I don't believe he would leave his sister alone after the shock she had."

"One moment, Nadia."

Hannah covered the phone, and I heard the murmur of

Jack, her husband's, voice. I'd met him once, but it was enough to recognize that he, too, was dangerous. They'd been on my side from the start. I wanted to remain there and be a part of the team, even if I was only connected via Hannah. There were others. Chris Shaw was another one I'd had contact with, but Hannah hadn't brought me fully into the fold. Someday, I hoped that she would. Their group wasn't like anything I'd ever experienced before. I wanted that.

The reception cleared as Hannah took her hand from the speaker. I appreciated that she hadn't muted it, which said more than she could have verbally. She did everything with a purpose, as did I. Those skills had been ingrained in us from the start.

"What is Cade to you, Nadia? Can you walk away?" she asked.

"Why are you asking me that?" I didn't understand. She knew from all those hours when she'd interrogated me, and I wondered whether it was a test.

"I've known you for six years and have watched you grow over that time. You came to us because of Cade. That was the turning point for you. I'll ask you again. Can you walk away from him?"

"No." I finally got what she meant. "He's the one, if he can forgive me."

"Jack suggests that you two get engaged. If he marries you, then you both would be seen as less of a risk, as he would have some level of protection that way. Cade's family connections provide a rather impressive red flag regarding your relationship with the CIA. We think this would help."

"So if we're legally married, the CIA won't think we were double agents?"

"Not quite, but they would see your relationship in a different light because Cade was the trigger for you all those years ago. Think about it." She paused. "Jack and I will fly out from Maine in an hour to make sure you're safe."

"There's a chance I can stay here?" I couldn't believe what she was offering if Cade was on board. That was the problem —I wasn't sure he was.

"We'll determine that when we arrive. Stay in contact."

It was a chance, and one I was going to take.

9

CADE

A brisk breeze rustled the leaves overhead as I rushed down the path to the plot of land that I was torn about keeping. Beneath the canopy of green, the tumultuous gray clouds were hidden from view. The weather matched my thunderous mood.

Nadia hadn't been at home, as I'd asked her to be. Nor had she been in the back by the pool. If she had taken off... I didn't even want to contemplate the thought of her leaving the island. There was one more place she could be, and for her sake, I hoped she was there. I was angry.

I'd spent most of the night talking with my sister, and the trauma from Anna's captivity went bone deep—not to mention our father's betrayal to our family. It was more than my sister or my mom could take... And even though I wanted to, I was struggling to put the blame on Nadia's shoulders. I needed to hear her out.

Parting the fronds from several dwarf palm trees, I stepped into the clearing that separated the jungle from the beach. The adrenaline that'd been pumping through my body surged at the sight of Nadia silhouetted by the ocean. Wind whipped her long black hair around her head.

I leashed the urge to shout and made my way to her. Not even the rolling waves that crashed against the shore nor the whistling wind kept my presence a secret, and she turned. An invisible string seemed to attach us so that we were aware of one another. I scanned her features for any indication of what she was feeling or what she would reveal. The only hint of emotion was deep in her stormy blue eyes.

"Are you going to contact the authorities?" Her voice was cold and hard.

"I should"—I shook my head—"but no. I want to hear your explanation." Anna had more or less admitted that Nadia had hidden her to keep her safe in some way. It didn't mean she wasn't frightened of Nadia, but it was enough to give me hope and hear her out. "Is this why you wanted to keep anything that happened before the island out of our relationship? Because you were involved with my father? I can't believe I was so stupid. I thought we had something between us, but it's all a lie, isn't it?"

"That's not—no," she replied. "What you know of me here has been real. I never meant to hurt you or Anna."

"Really? Then why did you kidnap my sister?" *Shit—I didn't mean to take it there.* I stepped away from her and forced myself to take slow, even breaths. When I was calmer, logic trickled in to inform me of what she'd done for both Anna and me in the end. I was mad, but there was more to the story. "Tell me about Anna and why you held her captive."

"I will." She pressed her lips together, and a few seconds passed where it seemed as if she was weighing whether to say something or not. "I have a proposition for you, Cade. It's going to sound crazy, but it's the only way that I can share everything. Answer a question for me, and then I'll tell you about Anna."

"Go ahead." My entire body vibrated from mixed emotions, including the need to touch her, which was at odds with what my mind said. The two were in a constant push and pull that I forced myself to ignore.

"Are you or do you plan to contact your father?" she asked, startling me.

"What?" With a growl, I turned from her and walked to the waterline, staring out at the darkening horizon. I'd thought I was angry, but I wasn't even close. The wind pushed at me, urging me to turn back to Nadia. Through gritted teeth, I told her the truth, giving her a glimpse into the hell that was unleashed after the accident, including my confusion and my sense of deep-set anger and betrayal. "I grew up American. Imagine my fucking surprise when we were informed that my dad wasn't a U.S. citizen but in fact Russian. He was arrested as a Russian spy."

"Have you been in contact with him since?"

I turned to face her, the disgust at the situation and at the thought of communicating with my father turning into a bloody haze that coated my vision. "No. I want nothing to do with him. He tore my family apart. Then the authorities… We were innocent. Imagine learning your sister was kidnapped and it had something to do with your father. Getting run off the road by whom? His associates? I don't even know what happened back then because the details were top secret, and we couldn't be trusted. Do you have any idea what that did to us? To my mom and sister?"

She didn't answer, but I didn't expect her to. I wanted her to feel my family's pain because she was somehow very involved in how things had unfolded five years before.

"When my mom first met Stan," I continued, "the man she's engaged to, she wouldn't even meet him for coffee until she'd run a full background check. We can't trust anyone. That's what my father did to us. She called the goddamned CIA to make sure Stan wasn't a suspect. Then there was you—a connection to the night of the accident, when you saved my life. And from what Anna says, she thinks you may have saved her in a roundabout way too. Explain that to me." Air sawed in and out of my lungs as I worked to maintain control, to stop myself from yelling at her or physically shaking her, trying to demand that she tell me what the hell her part had been in my family's fallout.

"You were my mark, Cade. Anna, too, but it was *you* who changed everything."

She slipped her hands into the pockets of her dark-gray drawstring pants.

I suddenly got a grip on my emotions for long enough to look at her, to see the turmoil she was experiencing, too, through her outfit of a white tank top that clung to her body and the cotton drawstring pants paired with black flip-flops. Her normally shiny hair was a mass of tangles. Even though she kept her emotions in check, hidden from view, her messy outer appearance told me she'd suffered the last night too. It settled some of the anger and confusion so I could listen to her.

"You were both supposed to die that night," she said quietly. "Anna at the hands of the people I lived with, and you... at mine."

"Were you working with my father? Did he order our deaths?"

"No."

I ran my hands through my hair. "Christ, Nadia. You were *seventeen* and supposed to *kill* me? Why?"

"I want to tell you, Cade, but I can't. Not unless..."

"What?" I took a step toward her, my fingers curling at my sides. I wanted to reach out, but I knew I shouldn't. I wondered why I was so willing to forgive her. A part of me trusted her with my life—she'd saved me. But I needed to understand, at the very least for my sister's sake.

"This is going to sound crazy." She inched closer, and I mirrored her movements. "I can't tell you everything unless"—her blue eyes met and held mine—"we're married."

* * *

Nadia

MY HEART WAS BEATING SO QUICKLY and furiously that I half expected my ribs to crack. He had to have thought I was crazy. I mean, I was, but at the same time, I'd meant what I'd asked him, and there was no one else who meant what he did to me.

I had to make him understand. "I'm not supposed to share this with you, Cade, but you deserve to know before you answer." I waited until he nodded. "I defected, and you're the reason why."

"Defected." His lip pulled back in a sneer. "From Russia?"

I yanked my hands from my pockets and threw them into the air in disgust, wanting to push him a little to get a reaction, to shake him up and pull him out of his sense of obligation to Anna, which was obviously clouding how he felt about me and about what we'd cultivated over the past few weeks. "Don't look at me like that. You're half Russian. What I've told you goes to your grave."

"Is that a threat?" he growled.

I ignored how his tousled hair made me want to run my fingers through it and curled my fingers in so that my nails left little half-moons in my palms. His expression was fierce, and he towered over me not in violence, but in protection. I'd noted the way he'd angled his shoulders, shielding me from the wind. Even if he wasn't ready to admit it to himself, his body unconsciously showed me what was in his heart. The feelings he had for me were not dead, just buried.

I hadn't meekly followed the orders from my handlers all those years before. I ran. But with Cade, I would hold my ground and fight for yet another thing I wanted. If he walked away, I would accept the consequences. I would relocate and face my life alone.

Wind howled through the trees as neither of us spoke. Taking another risk, I closed the distance between us and rested my head against his chest. My arms wrapped around his waist. I waited. Seconds ticked by before he gave in and engulfed me in his embrace. It was a small victory, a step toward bridging the cavern his sister's revelation had opened between us.

"What the hell am I going to do with you, Nadia?" His husky words sent a thrill along my exposed skin.

"Marry me."

"I would've asked you myself in another week or two if my sister hadn't shown up and exposed who you are to my family. Now, I need to know everything before I give you my answer. And Nadia?"

I leaned back enough to see his expression.

"I'll be the one asking."

I laughed because he'd basically admitted we would be okay. Everything would work out. I pulled out my cell and shot off a quick text to Hannah, asking her to wait to fly out and telling her that I'd call soon.

With my gut saying I could trust him, I went against my orders and told him everything. I explained how I'd grown up in America since I was eight years old but that I'd never been a child but a trained operative for Russia, transplanted to America as a sleeper agent, a spy. My handlers had lived in Canada for years undercover and had been charged to take me on as their child before moving to New York.

"Did you know my father?" he asked.

"I didn't. He was like me, though, like my handlers." I placed my palm over his heart, wishing I could ease his pain as fat drops of rain fell from the sky and splashed on my upturned face. "I'm sorry you were hurt."

His Adam's apple bobbed a few times. "They were going to deport us, but my mom was born and raised in New York and had never traveled to or anywhere near Russia. That's what enabled us to keep our citizenship. If she'd gone to Russia, even once on a layover, we would have been sent there." His arms tightened. "Why are you free, even if you defected?"

Despite the rain that was increasing in intensity, we remained locked in each other's arms, and I shared one more truth with him that held a chance of making him run for the hills. "I work for a woman who is connected to a special program in the CIA. I'm still an agent, just not for Russia."

10

CADE

The sound of insects carried on the warm breeze as I walked along the trail to Nadia's house at a few hours past dusk. I dragged my palm over my gritty eyes. It'd been a long three days with Anna, but it had also been a time of healing, so it was needed. Nadia and I focused on helping my sister overcome her fears from that dark time in my family life. Not only that, but Anna and Nadia were on their way to becoming friends, which was something I hadn't thought possible.

Leaves rustled overhead as I stepped up to Nadia's door and entered the passcode she'd given me. Once inside, I found her immediately in our favorite place, curled up on a chair by the pool. The slider was open, and she turned to greet me with her dark hair fanned around her. In her dark-gray drawstring pants and white camisole, she looked either ready for bed or for a serious talk.

Bed would come later, despite how much I wanted to pick her up and carry her to our bedroom. I'd checked out of the resort after Anna had left, and Nadia had moved me in while I'd taken my sister to the airport. We were both ready for the next chapter in our lives, but not without an in-depth discussion.

"I poured you a glass of whiskey," she said.

I laughed as I dropped onto the chair beside her. With my legs stretched out, I took a sip of the smooth Irish whiskey. "This is a precursor to what you're going to share with me?"

"Well, it'll help." She set her vodka down and took a deep breath. "You cannot under any circumstance discuss any of this to anyone other than me or reveal it to Hannah and Jack when they come here."

"They're aware that you're going to bring me in, though." I had to be clear. It had been my only stipulation to her proposal. I wanted there to be no secrets between us before we were married.

"Yes. I can tell you everything once we're legally married."

"Tell me about Hannah and Jack." They would be there in two weeks and needed to understand how they would fit into Nadia's life—and possibly mine.

A small smile touched Nadia's lips before it fell away. "Hannah was assigned to work with me when I turned myself in to the CIA with contingencies."

"What do you mean by that?"

She held my gaze and dropped her shields. *Goddamn.* Everything she was feeling was reflected in those deep-blue eyes, and I took her hand in mine, wanting to link us together by touch.

"The two Russian agents I lived with, who had the role of being my parents, were tasked with extracting an incriminating list from your father." She squeezed my hand to stop my next question. "Your father was the one who gave us passports, IDs, whatever we required when we had to disappear or assume new identities. Instead of staying true to the cause, he tried to blackmail the agents here to give him money, or he would leak our information."

I didn't think it was possible, but the hatred I had for my father grew. "We were aware of his duties afterwards, but we were not told about the evidence or the blackmail. Some of the questioning that we had to answer over and over again makes sense now."

She shrugged. "I'm sure it wasn't pleasant." She took a breath. "To how I know Hannah—when I went into the CIA, I told them I bargained with them to stay out of jail and to help you."

"Why?" We hadn't met before the accident, and even though she'd visited me in my dreams, our paths hadn't physically crossed until we were on the island together.

"It was this"—she gestured between us—"this strange connection we have. You and Anna were my marks to use against your father. The other two agents were tracking his movements, trying to figure out where he'd hidden the list and the best way to intercept him. He'd had the same training we did and was able to evade us. It was clear that Anna wouldn't have access to anything, and she was easy to subdue. It was safer for her too. They wanted you both killed. I could keep an eye on her and get her out when the time was right. It wasn't until the accident—"

"You could have kidnapped me too. I'm not following why you didn't." After that stunt when I'd surprised her when she was sleeping, I had no doubt she could have taken me down, regardless of how much bigger I was.

"We believed you might have had information, and I was to monitor everything you did. That lasted for two weeks." She traced circles on the back of my hand with her thumb. "I can't explain it, but there was a connection when I first saw you that went beyond looks. It was like my soul recognized you. It was a turning point for me, a way to get out, especially since I had a bargaining chip for the CIA."

"The list of names."

"Yes. Your father kept a list of all the Russian agents and what identities they assumed. There were so many… I went to the CIA and demanded to get assigned to a handler, to defect and work for a specialized team. There had to be something, and I wanted to be a part of it. I had no ties to my birthplace. I thought I was unique in how I felt about my life there before the one here, but I wasn't. That's when I was introduced to Hannah." Nadia shivered, and dark shadows moved in her eyes. "Hannah interrogated me in a way Russia had never trained me for. The method at the beginning, I was familiar with, but the duration and the biological agents she used… I had no reference in dealing with those. She broke me."

My hand tightened on hers. "Why do you work with her if she did that to you?" Nadia didn't appear broken in any way. She was the strongest person I knew, and that was only what she'd let me get a glimpse of.

"It was the only way she would bring me in. I accepted what she had to do and even understood. If it hadn't been for her, I wouldn't have the life I do now."

"I'm still confused about why Anna was taken but I was not." There was more to our story, so I pressed.

"The morning of your accident, we overheard a phone call from your father. He'd gotten sloppy. We'd put a tremendous amount of pressure on him. He was going to run, but you'd taken his keys."

"I remember. He called… He was furious. I'd misplaced mine, and since he was working from home that day, I swiped his. It wasn't the first time, and I couldn't understand what the big deal was." That argument we'd had seemed like a lifetime ago. It was the last time I'd spoken to my dad, and a small part of me regretted the words we'd exchanged.

"That clued us in to where he must have hidden the infor-mation, which was something one of his keys would have accessed. We tampered with your seatbelt to jam it when you started driving. The two agents I lived with ran you off the road. I was to swim to your car, break the window, and get the keys."

"You didn't do what you were supposed to, did you?" I remembered everything about that night, but not Nadia taking the keys.

A wide grin curved her mouth. "Oh, I got the keys, but I didn't let you die."

I would never forget that night for as long as I lived.

"Hannah was waiting for me when I got out of the river. I gave her the keys after she confirmed that your sister had been rescued."

"After that, they let you go? There weren't any repercussions, jail time, nothing?"

She shook her head. "I gave them the means to get the list of agents and aliases as well as three active ones hand delivered. So no. I didn't have any repercussions. Hannah vouched for me and brought me on to work for her."

Sensing her story was ending soon, I pulled her onto my lap. She rested her head on my chest, and I rubbed circles on her back. "Do you go on missions?"

"Not now. In the future, I'm sure I will have to, but for the time being, both Hannah and Jack think there could be other agents searching for me. It's not safe. So I work remotely, searching for suspicious individuals. I give the data to Hannah, and it's followed up on through her."

"You've mentioned Jack a few times. I got that he's her husband, but how does he fit into things?"

"He's a former Navy SEAL and a member of Gray Ghost security, which is a special-ops team that does search-and-rescue missions, among other high-risk operations. Both he and Hannah will be here soon. Are you sure you're up for this, for everything?"

"I asked you to move in with me before I found out who you were or how you were connected to my family. I'm here, Nadia. My feelings about you have not changed, only my understanding and respect for who you've become."

With a push against my chest, she repositioned to straddle me. My hands fell to her waist as she cupped my face with one hand, the other flat on my pounding heart.

In agonizing increments, she lowered her face inches from mine. "I love you, Cade." Her breath feathered my lips, and I tugged her closer.

With no more secrets between us, we were free. "Not more than I love you, Nadia." I took her mouth in a kiss to steal her breath and to ignite the same fire in her that she did in me. From the moment we'd first met, she'd become every-thing to me, and I planned to enjoy every minute of the rest of my life with her.

———

Nadia

Two Weeks Later

THE SUN'S rays reflected off the crystal-clear blue waters on another gorgeous day on the island. I took a calming breath and forced my nerves to settle. Cade and I had spent hours talking, and I'd shared with him many things I wasn't supposed to—at least not until after the next few minutes. It was an exceptional day, one I'd never dreamed I would have had. A heartfelt smile curved my lips as I met Cade's bright-green gaze a few feet away. He wore white board shorts and stood by the official who would marry us.

We'd decided to have a casual beach wedding with only Hannah and her husband, Jack, in attendance. They were standing up for us and would bear witness to our union, both on paper and to the CIA.

My hair fell down my back in loose waves, with a small crown of braids circling my head. White tiare maori flowers were woven into the circlet. Instead of a dress, I wore a white bikini with a sheer wrap low on my hips. We were barefoot, and as I walked across the white sands, heated by the midday sun, my heart burst with how perfect everything was.

The sweeping melody of a Tchaikovsky violin concerto played softly over the lapping waves. Cade grinned as I drew closer. We'd agreed to keep our vows simple. When I stood next to him, facing the official, he linked our hands.

We turned and faced one another with our fingers intertwined, and I barely heard what the man said until it was time to repeat my vows back to Cade from the depths of my soul. I meant every word: in sickness and in health… to love and to cherish…

We also added a few: "Our paths crossed at the right moment, opening the door to a love that will stand the test of time. I'll walk hand in hand with you in this life and in the next, as a partner, a friend, a soulmate."

Cade bent and claimed my mouth, pulling me against him in a knee-weakening kiss that sealed us together as husband and wife.

If you enjoyed reading Moonlit Mirage as much as I did writing it, I hope you'll consider leaving a review. For edge of your seat action, check out Broken Circle, book one in the Gray Ghost romantic suspense thriller series: https://amymckinleyauthor.com/gray-ghost-series/

ACKNOWLEDGMENTS

Nadia's story was a fun one to write, and while short, is a stepping-stone into a new series that's percolating in my head. I can't wait to see where it goes and to share it with you. This won't be the last of Nadia and Cade.

Several people are always there for me every step of the way, and I'm beyond grateful for their support and encouragement. My husband and four kids are amazing. I'm very fortunate.

I have a wonderful team of editors. Taylor Anhalt always has a significant role in the development of each book. I loved her content edit and how she helped to shape this story into what it is today. I have an incredible team from Red Adept Editing. Kate B. has been editing for me for the past two years, and I'm so lucky to be working with her. She helps to make my stories better, gets my thought process, and is so much fun to work with. Then Taylor A. swoops in to smooth out all the bumps in the proofread.

My critique partners, Kristin Kisska and Emily Albright, who are amazing authors themselves, are always willing to jump into every book, and I value their creative input. I'm thankful to have them in my inner circle.

Maryellen Newton, I'm so grateful for all the Panera coffee sessions where we go over our goals and catch up. You're a wonderful friend and spot on beta reader.

T.E. Black Designs, who did the cover design and formatting, you are a dream to work with, and each project exceeds my expectations.

Last but certainly not least, a special thank you to all the bloggers and readers who have encouraged and helped me along the way, and who continue to make my dream a reality.

Thank you.

ABOUT THE AUTHOR

 **Amy McKinley** is the romantic suspense thriller author of the Gray Ghost Novels, the Moonlit Destination series, the Five Fates paranormal romance series, and several stand-alone titles. Her edge-of-your-seat books are filled with surprising twists and just the right amount of heat and danger. She lives in Illinois with her husband, two daughters, two sons, and three mischievous cats.

You can find her at www.AmyMcKinley.com